this

little  ORCHARD

book belongs to

....

....

ORCHARD BOOKS
96 Leonard Street, London EC2A 4XD
Orchard Books Australia
14 Mars Road, Lane Cove, NSW 2066
First published in Great Britain in 2000
Copyright © Nicola Smee 2000
The right of Nicola Smee to be identified
as the author and illustrator of this work has been asserted by her
in accordance with the Copyright, Designs and Patents Act, 1988.
A CIP catalogue record for this book is available from the British Library.
1 84121 125 7 (hardback)
1 84121 129 X (paperback)
1 3 5 7 9 10 8 6 4 2 (hardback)
1 3 5 7 9 10 8 6 4 2 (paperback)
Printed in Italy

Freddie visits the dentist

Nicola Smee

little 🍀 ORCHARD

Bear's never been to the dentist,
so he's coming with me for a check-up.

I show Bear the dentist's chair
which he can move up and
down like a see-saw!

I open my mouth very wide
for the dentist to check my
teeth. It doesn't hurt at all!

"Now I'm going to give your teeth a polish," says the dentist. "This will tickle a little!"

"Well done, Freddie. Your teeth are sparkling and clean," says the dentist. "Now let's have a look at Bear."

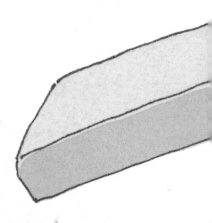

"Never mind, Bear," I say. "Have a rinse with this nice pink water."

When we leave, the dentist gives
me a new toothbrush. Bear
says HE wants one as well!

I must keep my teeth
brushed and clean,
the way the dentist showed me!

And I must keep my ears brushed and clean!